Night Mare

Backyard Horses

Dandi Daley Mackall

author of the bestselling Winnie the Horse Gentler series

Tyndale House Publishers, Inc.
Carol Stream, Illinois

Visit Tyndale's website for kids at www.tyndale.com/kids.

You can contact Dandi Daley Mackall through her website at www.dandibooks.com.

Night Mare

Designed by Jacqueline L. Nuñez

Edited by Stephanie Rische

For manufacturing information regarding this product, please call 1-800-323-9400.

Library of Congress Cataloging-in-Publication Data

Mackall, Dandi Daley.
Night mare / Dandi Daley Mackall.
p. cm. – (Backyard horses)
Summary: When someone claiming to be her horse's original owner shows up and wants the horse back, fourth-grader Ellie prays for a miracle.
ISBN 978-1-4143-3919-1 (sc)
[1. Horses–Fiction. 2. Loss (Psychology)–Fiction. 3. Christian life–Fiction.] I. Title. II. Title: Nightmare.
PZ7.M1905Ni 2012
[Fic]–dc23 2011040859

Printed in the United States of America

18 17 16 15 14 13
7 6 5 4 3 2

To Landri Claire Brigmon

Backyard horses are the opposite of show horses. They don't have registration papers to prove they're purebred, and they might never win a trophy or ribbon at a horse show. Backyard horses aren't boarded in stables. You can find them in pastures or in backyards. They may be farm horses, fun horses, or simply friends. Backyard horses are often plain and ordinary on the outside . . . but frequently beautiful on the inside.

☆ ☆ ☆

The Lord said to Samuel, "Don't judge by his appearance or height, for I have rejected him. The Lord doesn't see things the way you see them. People judge by outward appearance, but the Lord looks at the heart."

1 Samuel 16:7

1

Sunsets

Ellie James and her famous horse, Dream, have ridden for miles and miles. Ellie sits tall in the saddle, not looking like the shortest kid in fourth grade. Finally she sees the pet store, home of the international Pet Help Line. A crowd comes running out to greet Ellie and Dream. A tall boy with long hair shouts, "Far out! You made it, man! Groovy!" Ellie would recognize Catman Coolidge in a heartbeat, even if he weren't carrying four fat cats. And she knows at once that the dark-haired, freckle-faced girl next to him is Winnie the Horse Gentler. Winnie leaps onto her white Arabian, Nickers. Then Winnie and Ellie ride off into the sunset on Nickers and Dream.

Something hits me in the head, knocking me out of a great daydream and back into my classroom. I spot a paper wad on my desk. I don't have to look far to see who threw it. Colt Stevens, my most-of-the-time best friend.

I spread my hands apart, palms up. It's sign language for *What?* Colt and I learned sign language so we could talk to Ethan, my little brother. But knowing sign comes in handy at school, too.

Colt faces Miss Hernandez, our teacher. Then he sticks his hands behind his back and signs to me, *You're next.*

I touch my chin and bring my hand down,

signing, *Thanks.* Colt can't see me, but my mom says being thankful is like breathing. You might not notice when you're doing it, but you sure miss it when you aren't.

"Ellie and Cassie?" Miss Hernandez smiles our way. She has a great ponytail. It swishes behind her. After today, we only have one more day of school before summer will be here and Miss Hernandez won't be our teacher anymore. I'm going to miss her. One of the best things about our fourth-grade teacher is her ponytail. But there are lots of other best things too. Like her laugh. And the way she doesn't yell, even when she's mad. And how she doesn't make us feel stupid if our work isn't as good as somebody else's, like Larissa's.

Cassie stands up. She jerks her head for me to join her in front of the class.

I shake my head. "You're the spokeswoman," I remind her.

Cassie giggles, sounding a little nervous. "Ellie and I split the work on our blog project. Ellie collected all the recipes for horse treats. We made them together and tried them out on real horses. But Ellie did most of the work on the recipes. So you're stuck with me as spokeswoman."

The class laughs, in a nice way. Everybody loves Cassie. I'm lucky I got to be her partner for our final project–creating our own blog. The best thing about Cassie, besides that she has a horse named Misty, is that even though she's one of the most popular kids in our school, she doesn't act like it. When Miss Hernandez paired us up to develop a blog for our class project, Cassie seemed honest-to-goodness happy to be getting me for a partner.

"Well, it sounds as if you girls worked out your partnership very well," Miss Hernandez says.

Cassie smiles at me. "It was fun. Tell them how we came up with the idea, Ellie."

I feel my face turn hot. But I don't really mind telling this part. "You guys know how skinny my horse, Dream, used to be."

"No kidding!" Larissa says. "That pony looked like a scarecrow."

Larissa Richland is as tall as I am short. She thinks she knows everything about horses. But I don't see how she can know that much because she doesn't take care of her horse. She lets a fancy stable do everything for her. The best thing about Larissa is . . . well, I guess it's that maybe she won't be in my fifth-grade class next year.

"Larissa," Miss Hernandez says, "it's not your turn now, is it?"

"No, Miss Hernandez," Larissa answers. "But on *my* blog–I mean, Colt's and my blog–we're always looking for funny stories to tell. So we might want to write about how animal control had to chase that scraggly pinto all over the school lawn."

With her teacher stare, Miss Hernandez gets Larissa to stop talking. Only it's too late. Larissa already got my mind off track. Now all I can think about is the day I first saw my horse out this exact same school window. Everybody thought it was just my imagination. But it wasn't.

Who could have known that the skinny horse I saw that day would end up being my very own Dream?

"Ellie, please go on," Miss Hernandez says.

But I can't go on because I don't remember where I was.

Colt signs, *Skinny pinto, needed treats.*

"Right!" Now I remember. "Skinny. When I got Dream, she was so skinny you could see daylight through her. Not really. But that's how my mom put it. She also said my horse was so skinny she disappeared when she turned sideways."

Larissa fake gags.

"Once I brought Dream home, I had to fatten her up," I continue. "We used special feed, and that worked. But I started searching the Internet for horse treat recipes. Some were awful. They used peanut butter, and that's not great for horses. Then I found the coolest thing. A pet help line. Several kids get together to answer questions about animals. They've got this guy named Catman who knows everything about cats. And this kid Barker answers all the dog questions."

Larissa yawns. It's as loud as the fire alarm.

"Anyway, a girl named Winnie knows more about horses than anybody in the world, I'll bet."

"I'll bet," Larissa mutters.

I press on. "Her recipes for horse treats were the best."

Cassie takes over. "We're not using anything without permission. Winnie wrote back to Ellie and said she could use the recipes. We give Winnie credit on our blog. Plus, we blog about how our horses liked the treats."

"Good job, girls," Miss Hernandez says. She calls the next team and the next.

Larissa and Colt go last.

Larissa starts to get up, but Miss Hernandez stops her with that look again. "Colt, let's hear from you first. Tell us about your blog."

Colt looks like he wasn't counting on this. "Well, Larissa wanted to call it *Starring Larissa*, and I didn't care. So that's what it is. Her mom's helping us a lot with all the blog and computer stuff. She's got lots of ideas."

Miss Hernandez tugs her ponytail. "So your blog is about Larissa?"

Colt shrugs. He told me he didn't care what it was about. He just wanted school to end.

"It's not *just* about me," Larissa says. She stands and walks to the front of the room. "*Star-*

ring Larissa is fun, entertaining, and educational." She glances at her note cards. "Just click on 'The Larissa Show' and read about horse shows. You can see pictures of my trophies and ribbons. Click on 'Larissa's Logic' for advice about horses and anything else. Or read 'Larissa Laughs,' and you may find a good joke or story." She looks at me. "That's where I could write about Ellie's little pony."

Larissa knows Dream isn't a pony. She's a horse–a beautiful pinto horse. Larissa just calls her a pony to make me mad.

But too bad for Larissa. Even she can't get me upset on a day like this. There's too much to be thankful for. Tomorrow, Saturday, I'm going on a trail ride. Monday is the last day of school, thanks to only one extra snow day this winter.

Colt and I have better things to do than worry about a blog. Summer will be filled with trail rides, horse shows, early-morning breakfast rides, and moonlight horse strolls.

Nope. Even Larissa Richland can't mess up a summer like that.

2

Lucky

"Ellie, what rhymes with fish?" Dad asks. He looks up from his laptop, which sits on our dining room table.

Colt and my brother, Ethan, are sitting with me on one side of the table. Dad and his work junk are taking up the other side. Dad pretends our dining room is his office, unless we're eating in here.

"Lots of words rhyme with *fish*, Dad," I say.

"Anything remotely helpful or whatnot?" he asks, raking his hair with his fingers. The brown waves spread out all over his head. Dad looks like he's been dropped from a tornado. On his head. He only gets like this when he's stuck and in need of rhymes. My dad writes jingles for the Jingle Bells Ad Agency. If he doesn't come up with great ideas, his bosses might fire him. One of Dad's bosses is Colt's mom.

"What's the ad campaign, Mr. James?" Colt asks.

Dad slumps in his chair. He's pretty short, so slumping puts him at about our level. "It's the Fantastic Fish Food campaign. I had a funny jingle about flying fish and whatnot. But no, they want a rhyming jingle." He turns to me. I'm the ace rhymer in the family. "So, Ellie?"

"Fish," I repeat. I reach for a pen and knock over two cans of dog food. My mom talked Colt and Ethan and me into helping her with her Doggone Drive. We glue pictures of missing dogs on cans and pass them out in the neighborhood.

I pick up the tipped cans and start rhyming: "*Fish, dish, wish, squish–*"

The table jiggles. "Munch, easy," Colt says.

Ethan reaches under the table to pet his dog. Munch is the size of a miniature horse. And he's still growing. When he wags his tail, it feels like an earthquake.

I try again. "*Fish* is a harder rhyme than I thought, Dad."

"Tell me about it." He rests his head on the table.

"Okay." In my mind, I race through all possible *fish* rhymes. Nothing sounds worthy of a jingle. "Maybe we could go with fishy. Then we could use squishy and splishy, like splishy-splashy. Oooh! How about swishy? Like a horse's tail going swishy?" I always try to squeeze in at least one horse rhyme, no matter what the jingle.

Dad smacks his forehead on the table.

Ethan sets down the dog food can he's working on. He signs, *Isn't Mom at a fish protest today?*

Colt laughs. "I thought you said fish protest," he says, signing it too.

We don't laugh.

"Seriously?" Colt says. "Your mother is protesting fish?"

"I tried to talk her out of it," Dad says.

Colt glances around the table at Ethan and me. "You guys have to admit that's a little weird, right? Your dad's advertising for fish, and your mom's protesting them?"

"She's not protesting fish," I explain. "She's protesting *for* fish."

Colt already knows that my mom loves all animals. She's a professional volunteer. She works at a cat farm, a dog barn, a worm ranch, and lots of other places. "Have you ever seen the fish in that fake pond in front of the fish market?"

"I've never seen fish in that pond," Colt says.

"That's because the water is so scummy. Mom says the fish are dying. That's why she's protesting."

Munch barks. A second later the front door bangs open. My mom swirls into the dining room on roller skates, the antique kind that clamp to her shoes. One of the best things about my mom is that she never just walks into a place like regular people do. She bursts in like the sun.

"Hi, honey!" Dad sits up straight. He reminds me of Lance, a boy in my class. Whenever Ashley Harper walks by Lance, he brightens up like Christmas. Dad's that way every time he sees Mom.

Mom kisses Dad's head. Then she rounds the table and kisses all of our heads, even Colt's. "I'm so hungry I could eat the south end of a northbound skunk!" she declares.

My mother is wearing pastel-pink and blue

painter pants and a T-shirt with just about every other color on it. She tie-dyed the shirt herself.

"What's with the old-fashioned skates, Mrs. James?" Colt asks. "My sister likes to roller-skate. But she's got shoe skates. You know–all in one, with wheels on the boots."

Colt's sister, Sierra, moved to St. Louis with their dad when Colt's parents got a divorce. He hardly ever mentions her.

"Ah," Mom says, fingering a metal key on a string she wears around her neck. "But does your sister get to wear one of these?"

Colt squints at the old silver skate key. "You got me there. No key for Sierra."

"And there you have it." Mom plunks her orange patent leather handbag on the table and drops into the chair next to Dad. She crosses one leg over the other and starts unlocking her skates. "I'm tired as a squashed bug on a tractor tire." As if she just now noticed our handiwork, she picks up one of the dog food cans Ethan has finished. A collie named Lucky is on the can, along with a phone number. "Great job! These are pretty as a pumpkin! I'll pass them out tomorrow. We'll find Lucky before you know it." Mom winks at me.

I wink back. I think Lucky is lucky to have my mom on the case.

3

Surprises

How did the fish protest go, Mom? Ethan asks.

"I'm as forgetful as a frog in love!" Mom grabs her orange purse and pulls out a plastic sack of murky water and sets it on the table. "There you go, Ethan. Surprise!"

Ethan takes the bag. He peers into it, and his mouth drops open.

I lean over and stare into the bag too. "Mom, there are fish in there!" The bag smells like pond scum.

"I was only able to rescue three of the poor things. And I have to warn you, Ethan. Those fish are sick as an alligator in a shoe store. But I thought if anyone could nurse them back to health, it's Ethan James."

Colt and I search the attic until we come up with the little aquarium Dad bought me two years ago.

"Remember when your dad won that goldfish for you at the county fair?" Colt asks. "He had to throw quarters onto a plate, right?"

I nod. "Mom said we could have bought a boat with the quarters it took to win that fish. And the poor thing didn't even last one day."

Colt helps Ethan set up the tank while I bring in pitchers of water to fill it.

"What will you name them?" Colt asks Ethan.

Ethan shrugs. He sets the plastic bag of fish into the tank water. That way the fish can get used to their new home before leaving the old murky water.

"What kind of fish are they?" Colt asks.

"Goldfish," Mom answers. She hands Ethan a small can of fish food.

"Goldfish?" I stare into the fish tank. All three fish are gray and shriveled up. "They don't look gold. They look charcoal. Like somebody had a fish fry . . . and they were the guests of honor."

That's it! Ethan signs. His fingers move at lightning speed. *They do look burned. So I think I'll name them Shadrach, Meshach, and Abednego.*

"What did you say?" Colt squints at Ethan's fingers.

Ethan finger-spells the names again.

"I have no idea what you're spelling, Ethan," Colt complains.

"Shadrach, Meshach, and Abednego," I say. I'm

glad I can say it instead of spelling it. Ethan's only in second grade, but he's a better speller than I am.

Colt scrunches his eyebrows. "I still don't get it. Who are Shad and Me-whatever and Bednego?"

Colt's mother doesn't take him to church. Neither does his dad when he goes to St. Louis to see him. Every time we've asked Colt to go to church with us, his mom says he can't.

I explain as much as I can remember from Sunday school about Shadrach, Meshach, and Abednego. "They were three Old Testament guys who were captured by a mean king. The king tried to make them pray to an idol instead of to God. When they wouldn't, the king threw them into the lions' den."

Ethan shakes his head. *Daniel got thrown into the lions' den. Daniel's friends*–Ethan nods to the fish–*were thrown into the fiery furnace.*

"I get it," Colt says. He presses his nose against

the fish tank. "These fish do look like they've been through the fire, all right." He looks back to Ethan. "Did they die? The Bible guys, I mean?"

Ethan grins and shakes his head again. *They prayed, and God rescued them. They didn't even smell like smoke when they got out of the furnace.* Ethan strokes the tank as if he's petting his new fish.

Before Colt has to go home, we go to Ethan's room to check our blogs. Ethan and I share a computer. Last month I had the computer in my room. This month it's in Ethan's room. My brother's room screams "Baseball!" He pitches for his baseball team, and he has pictures of famous pitchers covering one wall. His throw rug is a big, fluffy baseball. And his bed is covered with a Kansas City Royals blanket.

Colt takes Ethan's desk chair and checks the *Starring Larissa* blog. "Man, Larissa and her mom have added a ton of stuff since this morning."

"I still can't believe you let Larissa get away with that blog name, Colt."

He ignores me and keeps squinting at the screen.

While I'm waiting on Colt, I take out my blog folder and thumb through some of the recipes. Winnie the Horse Gentler gave me a great idea for a treat you don't have to cook. I'm going to change the recipe a little and call it Molasses Monster Munch. But my favorite recipe is for Oat and Apple Bars. Cassie and I made two dozen of them. Dream would have eaten every last bar if we'd have let her.

Colt groans. "Ellie, you better read this."

"A blog starring Larissa? No thanks. I get enough Larissa at school."

"I'm serious, Ellie. Get over here."

Something in Colt's voice makes me walk over to the computer. The first thing I see is an old picture of my horse. The dirty, scraggly pinto in that photo hardly looks like Dream. Her ribs are sticking out, and her ears are flat back.

"Leave it to Larissa to post the worst possible picture of Dream," I say. "But so what? I'm not going to let her get to me." I turn my back on the screen.

"I'm not talking about the picture," Colt says. "Or her version of the story." He frowns at me. "I'm talking about the comments, Ellie."

"What comments?" I don't like the way my stomach feels, like it's tangled inside.

"Well, there are a bunch of dumb comments after the story. Somebody wrote that he didn't think the picture was real because the horse looks like a scarecrow. Somebody else tried to make a joke about 'backyard horses' being 'backward horses.'"

Whenever anybody says something mean

about Dream, it turns me into a cross between a bucking bronco and a wild mustang. But Dream doesn't even look like that picture now. "Colt, who cares what strangers have to say about an old picture?"

But Colt isn't finished. He's still staring at the screen, still shaking his head. "It's this last comment, Ellie. You better read it."

"You read it." What could somebody say that hasn't been said already?

"Okay." Colt glances at me one more time. Then he reads the comment. "It says: 'Hey! The horse in that picture–that's my horse!'"

4

No Comment!

I stare at the computer screen. My fingers grip the chair so I don't fall down. The words blur together: *Hey! The horse in that picture–that's my horse!*

"Are you okay, Ellie?" Colt asks.

I can't answer him. I can't take my gaze off the final two words in the comment: *my horse!*

Before I realize what I'm doing, I'm screaming, "No!" Then I shout even louder, "Mom! Dad! Mom! Dad!"

My parents thunder up the stairs and into Ethan's room.

"Ellie?" Dad says. "What on earth . . . ?"

Mom strides to the computer in two steps. "I'll be a mummy's mummy if you didn't scare ten years off my life. What's so catawampus that you had to ruin a perfectly good rerun of *Saved by the Bell*?"

"Ellie read something on Larissa's blog and freaked out," Colt explains.

"The freaked-out part we got," Mom says.

"What's on the blog?" Dad asks. "Aren't you doing a blog with Cassandra?"

"Read it." My voice sounds like I'm under murky water. A dying fish. That's how I feel–like I'm drowning in pond scum. I can hardly move. Mom and Dad have to crowd in to get a better look at the computer screen.

"Is that Dream?" Dad asks, pointing to the old picture. "I almost forgot how sickly your horse was before we got her." He scrolls up a little. "Is that Larissa's horse?"

I glance at the photo. Larissa is holding a trophy. Next to her is her American saddle horse, Custer's Darling Delight.

"The one on the right is Larissa's horse," Colt informs Dad. "The one on the left is Larissa."

Mom chuckles. "Well, that Larissa has a way with words, all right. She got the story wrong. But it's kind of funny. You shouldn't take it so personally, Ellie."

"It's not the story we're worried about," Colt explains. "It's the comments. The last comment."

I watch Mom's eyes narrow as she reads.

"I'll be a blue-nosed gopher," she mutters.

Dad is reading through the comments too. His eyebrows shoot up and down like the wings of a bird trying to take off. "It has to be a joke or whatnot," he finally says.

"Do you think so, Mr. James?" Colt asks.

"Must be," Dad answers.

Mom slaps Dad on the back. "You are the smartest man I know, Lenny James! Of course it's a joke. A very bad joke." Mom looks totally relieved.

I want to believe them. *I* want to feel relieved. "But what if it's not a joke?" I demand. "What if whoever had Dream before she showed up at the cat farm really did recognize her from Larissa's blog?"

My mind flashes back to the day when I saw the shaggy pinto from my classroom window. Nobody else saw her there. And by the time Colt and I walked home from school, he almost had me believing the horse was all in my imagination. Then Mom came home from volunteering at the cat farm and announced she'd lost a stray spotted horse. And that was the beginning of my dream come true.

Mom puts her arm around me. She has to bend in half to look me in the eyes. "Sugar, whoever had that poor horse before you got her wouldn't likely be admitting it." She points toward the picture on the screen. "Who would confess to starving a horse like that? Why, I'd arrest him myself for being cruel to animals. He'd be hog-tied and strung up in a court of law."

"Your mom's got a point, Ellie," Colt says.

"She always does," Dad agrees.

"Hey!" Colt scoots his chair up to Ethan's desk again. "I'm going to comment on the comment."

"Can you do that?" Dad asks.

"This is my blog too," Colt says. "I got teamed with Larissa for the blog project."

"And you call it *Starring Larissa*?" Mom asks.

Colt types, and the rest of us read his comment as he goes along: *Oh yeah? This is NOT your horse. And even if you did own this horse once, you better not admit it. They put people in jail for starving horses.*

"There!" Colt leans back in the chair and clicks

the button to post it. Only Colt's comment doesn't show up. Instead, he gets a message back that says, "Thank you for your comment. All comments must be approved by Larissa. Have a nice day!"

"That stinks!" Colt shouts.

It's at that moment when I get it. "Yes! I should have thought of that right off. It's Larissa!"

"What do you mean, honey?" Dad asks.

"That comment! Don't you get it? I'll bet you anything Larissa is the one writing all the comments on her site." I can picture her sitting at home making up every word. "*She's* the one calling Dream a scarecrow. She's the one making fun of backyard horses. And she's the one trying to stir up trouble by claiming *my* horse is really *her* horse."

"Well, I'll be a four-toed fiddler," Mom mutters.

"I guess," Colt says. "I know she and her mother were worried that nobody would see the blog. Larissa really wanted people to write comments."

"See? I'm right!" I'd love to send Larissa a few comments of my own right now.

"So when she didn't get any comments, she must have decided to write them herself," Colt says, like he's thinking aloud.

Dad sighs and backs away from the computer. "If this crisis is over, then I guess I'd better get back to my own crisis. Fish rhymes."

"I'll help," Mom offers, even though she once tried to rhyme *bowling* with *sewing*. That jingle almost got Dad fired.

☆ ☆ ☆

After Colt leaves, I fill Ethan in on Larissa's blog. He makes me find the website so he can read it for himself. When he's done, he signs, *Are you sure Larissa wrote that comment?*

I make a fist and wave it up and down at him, signing, *Yes!* But I wish he hadn't asked.

Ethan shakes his head. *That's awfully mean, even for Larissa. You'd better take the computer to your room so you can keep an eye on her blog.*

After we move the computer into my room, Ethan and I check on Shadrach, Meshach, and Abednego. They're still alive, but they're not swimming much.

By the time I'm ready for bed, I'm pretty tired. I open my bedroom window and call, "Dream!" Stars are just starting to light up the sky.

In seconds I hear my horse's hoof beats and know she's trotting toward me. Dream appears at the edge of the yard, tossing her head. Her white mane floats across her neck. Dream doesn't stop until she's at my window.

When Dad and I fenced in our backyard, we decided one side of the fence would be our house.

That's why my bedroom window opens up into Dream's pasture–our yard.

Dream nickers and sticks her head in through the window so I can pet her. I sit on the window ledge, and my horse stretches her neck until her head rests in my lap. When I scratch her jaw, her eyes droop shut.

"You're mine, Dream. All mine."

I usually say my going-to-bed prayers when I'm in bed. But I'm so wound up from Larissa's blog that I decide I'll say my prayers with Dream tonight. "God, thanks for helping Dream and me find each other." I thank God for Ethan and Mom and Dad and Colt and Cassie and everybody else I can think of. Only not Larissa.

"Dream," I whisper when I'm done talking to God, "you and I have a lot to be thankful for, including that trail ride tomorrow."

I kiss Dream good night and watch her trot

off in the starlight. Then I curl up in bed and try to sleep. Only I'm so excited about the trail ride, sleep stays away for a long, long time.

Just when I start drifting off, I jerk myself awake because I'm starting to have a nightmare. In my dream, Larissa is taking *my* horse and handing her over to some stranger.

And then I can see Ethan's hands signing, *That's awfully mean, even for Larissa.*

5

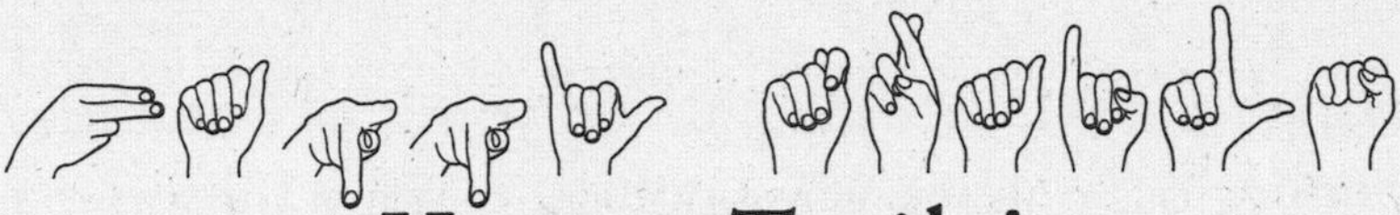

Happy Trails!

The sun is barely rising when I open my window and whistle. A cool breeze sweeps into my bedroom, and with it the sweet scent of horse. Dandelions have popped up all across the yard. Dew sparkles in patches of clover.

Dream canters up to the window, and I give her a good morning kiss right on her blaze. "Trail ride today, Dream. We're going to have so much fun. Hang on. I'll get your breakfast."

I pull on jeans and a T-shirt. On the way out

of my room, I notice the computer. So I stop and check my e-mail. All junk, except for one from Winnie the Horse Gentler. I open it right away.

Happy trails, Ellie! Have fun on your trail ride today. I ran across one more recipe you might want for your blog project. Nickers loves these treats, and they're easy to make.
Nickers's Noshes
1 cup flour
2 cups oatmeal
3 cups unsweetened applesauce

Preheat oven to 350 degrees.
Grease a 13-inch pan and pour in mixture.
Bake for about 40–45 minutes. Cool completely before giving a piece to your horse.

I copy the recipe. Then I write Winnie a thank-you note before heading to the backyard.

My dad is already hard at work in his dining room office. "Ellie, what are you doing up so early on a Saturday?"

"Trail ride. Remember?" I walk over to him. Stacks of papers litter the whole table. Paper wads cover the floor like giant snowflakes. "Tough night, Dad?"

"A rhyme-less night, if that's what you mean."

I feel sorry for my dad. I'm about to go on the most fun ride ever, and he's stuck at home trying to rhyme *fish.* I start to sit down in the chair next to Dad, but Squash, our cat, is curled up there.

"Hey, Dad. How about this?

"There's nothing fishy about our food.
We'll put your fish in the very best mood!"

"Yes!" Dad exclaims. "I can work with that. I need to put in the name of the company, of course. And a tune and whatnot. . . ."

I leave Dad to his jingle, and I rush out back

to give Dream her oats. Pinto Cat, the calico who followed Dream and me home from the cat farm and decided to stay, demands her food too. While Dream eats, I brush her. "So, Dream, what do you think about riding bareback today?"

Dream keeps eating and acts like she doesn't hear the question.

"You've filled out enough. I can ride you bare-back now without killing myself on your bony spine." I give her back an extra brushing. Instead of her bone sticking up there, she has a nice, padded, broad back now. I love my horse's spots. I brush my favorite spot, the one that looks like a shiny black saddle. "You know, Dream, this saddle spot looks like God drew it on you Himself."

When Dream is finished eating, I lead her over to my mounting post, a tree stump we already had in the backyard. Even standing on the stump, I have to jump a little to get up on her back.

"You are so not a pony," I tell her. "Once again, Larissa doesn't know what she's talking about."

Dream and I trot across the road to Colt's. I expect to have to wake him up for the ride. But Colt is already in the barn, with his horse saddled and ready to go.

"Wow! Bullet looks great, Colt. He's thinned down a lot."

"I think so too," Colt says. "See?" He pulls back the big stirrup of his Western saddle to show me the cinch buckle. "Two notches tighter than the last time I rode with this saddle."

Bullet still needs to lose another three or four notches. But it's progress. It has taken me a long time to fatten up Dream. I suppose it will take Colt a long time to "skinny down" Bullet.

"I think we can get into some serious barrel racing this summer," I say.

"Counting on it." He unties Bullet and leads

him out of the barn. Colt mounts his horse from the left, the way we learned in horsemanship. He lands on Bullet's back with a thud.

I bite my tongue to keep from telling him he needs to grab a bit of the mane from the base, along with the reins, in his left hand. And he should face the back of his horse and take hold of the cantle, or the back of the saddle, with his right hand. That way he could bounce on his right foot, with his left in the stirrup. That would help him spring into the saddle without thumping down so hard.

I only know these things because I've been going to Mr. Harper's horsemanship classes forever, long before I had my own horse. But today isn't for the how-tos of horsemanship. It's for the sheer joy of riding. That's what Mr. Harper said when he invited us to his property for the trail ride.

"Let's go," I say, reining Dream around.

Colt and I ride side by side down our road.

Our homes are the last two houses on this end of town. I love living out here, where our yards are the size of most people's pastures.

The gravel road turns to dirt. Wildflowers peek out from ditches on both sides. I spot tiny sweet clover. "Colt, do you remember when we used to pull out the purple from those clovers and try to taste the sugar?"

He laughs. "You always claimed you could taste it, but I never did."

A cardinal zooms right in front of us, but neither horse shies at it. It's like the birds are as excited about our trail ride as we are. We pass pastures of black-and-white cows. Before long, the only sounds are the clip-clop of hooves and the squeak of Colt's leather saddle.

"I heard from Larissa this morning," Colt says.

"What did *she* want?"

"She wanted me to come to her house and

help with the blog instead of going on the trail ride." Colt reaches down and pats Bullet. That's one of the best things about Colt. He treats his horse like he's a best friend. "I told her thanks, but no thanks."

"Did she say anything about the comments on her blog?" I know Larissa wrote those things. But my stomach still flips over just remembering that half a second when I thought somebody else wrote that comment.

"I asked her about it. She acted like she didn't know what I was talking about." Colt glances at me. "But she did. She just didn't want to admit we're onto her."

I remember my nightmare. And for a second, worry creeps like a cockroach up the back of my neck.

Neither of us says anything for a while.

I shake off my nightmare and refuse to think

about Larissa. I'm glad she'll be home working on that blog of hers instead of riding on the trail with us. Larissa's horse lives at K. C. Stables. Maybe she didn't think it was worth the hassle of having somebody drive her horse to the Harpers'. Custer's Darling Delight wouldn't do so well on a trail ride anyway. He's used to practice arenas, not forest trails.

But I'm done thinking about Larissa.

Colt is quiet, but I never worry about making small talk with him. That's one of the best things about Colt and me, most of the time. We don't have to be talking to know everything's okay between us.

"This is my first trail ride," Colt says when the Harpers' stable appears in the distance.

"Mr. Harper took us on a trail ride for an hour last year, out at Brookfield," I say. "But this one will be way better. And longer."

Colt reaches behind his saddle and pats his saddle bags. "That's why I packed enough food for the whole day."

I stare at his saddle bags. I thought they were just decoration. "Um . . . I didn't think about that. I haven't packed anything."

"No sweat." Colt strokes Bullet again. "I made plenty of peanut butter sandwiches. I even made those apple-carrot horse treats from your blog. Bullet will share with Dream. Won't you, boy?"

"Well, Dream and I both thank you two." And I know right away this day is going to be something I'll never forget.

Only just as I think this, I feel that worry-cockroach crawling back up my neck. I stare at the blue sky and bright sun. But I imagine a black cloud lurking over the horizon. And I'm pretty sure that nasty cloud is Larissa-shaped.

6

Joy

Mr. Harper waves to us as we ride up. He's busy leading three of his horses to a hitching post. The Harpers have so many horses that Mr. Harper always lets kids who don't have horses ride some of his.

That was me for a long, long time. Every horsemanship practice I'd ride one of the Harper horses because I didn't have a horse of my own. I shoot up a prayer of thanks to God that now I have Dream.

Ashley Harper comes yawning out of the barn. She's wearing jeans and a T-shirt like me. Only she looks like she's stepped off the cover of a fashion magazine. She shields her eyes from the sun and then waves.

"Hey, Ashley!" I call. "Which horse are you taking out?"

She holds up one finger, then jogs back to the barn. When she comes out, she's leading Galahad, a young quarter horse that has already won three ribbons.

Mr. Harper takes off his cowboy hat and wipes his forehead with the back of his hand. "Can you believe that girl nearly forgot her horse?" he asks.

I'm not sure Ashley would ride if it weren't for her dad taking her to the shows. She doesn't love horses the way Colt and I do.

I'm surprised when Rashawn walks out of the barn behind Ashley and Galahad. Rashawn's coal-black hair is caught up in a clip that matches the clip in Ashley's long blonde hair.

Rashawn is leading her horse, Dusty. Next to Galahad, Rashawn's farm horse looks like a giant. She tries to get Dusty to hurry up, but that horse has a mind of her own.

"What are you doing here already?" I ask Rashawn. "I thought you and Cassie would ride over together."

"My fault," Ashley says. She yawns again. "Rashawn and I are so far behind on our blog that she had to stay over last night so we could work on it. I'm a terrible partner."

"No, you're not," Rashawn says. "We got a lot done yesterday." Rashawn is a great student, and she always works hard. I haven't heard her complain once about Ashley not doing her share of the work.

"How on earth did you and Colt get here so early?" Ashley asks.

Colt grins. "Our horses are lightning fast."

"Anybody want to give me a hand here?" Mr. Harper shouts.

Colt helps Mr. Harper saddle the horses he's letting people use while Ashley saddles Galahad.

I follow Rashawn back to the barn and help her with Dusty. Once we're out of earshot, I quiz her. "What was it like staying at Ashley's?"

"Aside from the fact that her room is bigger than my whole house, you mean?" Rashawn laughs. "It was cool. You should see her room. Seriously. She has a king-sized guest bed–for *moi*. I had to beg Ashley to show me her trophies. She keeps them in a trunk. And she doesn't have her ribbons hanging on the wall like Larissa does."

I've never seen Larissa's or Ashley's rooms. "What else did you do?"

"We really did work on our blog. The project would have been easier if Ashley hadn't begged me to stay away from anything related to horses. So we're doing presidential candidates. Neither of us knows anything about that one. Or cares. That's the problem."

It takes both of us to brush Dusty and hoist the saddle onto her back.

"There you are!" Cassie runs up to us. She's leading her pony. At 14 hands, Misty is a true pony, and Cassie is fine with that . . . except when Larissa calls Misty Phony Pony.

"Cassie!" Rashawn hugs her friend and launches into a detailed account of her overnight with Ashley.

After a minute, I slip out of the barn and back to Dream. My horse is standing all by herself. I look around for Colt and Bullet. Finally I spot them on the other side of the stable with Lance and Brendon. Brendon only comes to horsemanship a few times a year. Lance doesn't even like horses. He only shows up at horsemanship events because he knows Ashley will be there.

But they're the only other guys here. So I know Colt will want to hang with them.

Mr. Harper has us line up. "A few rules before we start. Rule number one: You're not the only one on this ride. Look out for each other. Rule number two: Stay on the trail unless I give you the go-ahead to explore. Rule number three: Keep a horse's length between you and the horse in front of you. Rule number four: Have fun, riders!"

Cassie and Rashawn fall in right behind Mr. Harper. Cassie turns in her saddle and shouts back, "Ellie! Come on up here with us."

Rashawn nods and waves me up too.

That's one of the best things about Cassie and Rashawn. Even though they're best friends with each other, they always try to include me.

I glance around for Ashley. She's the last rider

in the pack. I wave to her. But she has her head down on her horse's neck like she's taking a nap.

Mr. Harper leads us through two of his pastures and out to the woods. The trail is covered by a blanket of pine needles and spreads between jagged rows of evergreens. Our horses' hooves sound like they're in stocking feet, swishing across a silk carpet. Sunlight flashes between the branches. The scent of pine mixes with horse, smelling so good I'm a little dizzy.

"Is all of this your land?" Cassie asks Mr. Harper.

"This part is," he answers. "But we're headed over that ridge into woods that are publicly held. I love these woods."

"Me too," I whisper, so low that nobody can hear me except Dream and God. I feel as much pure joy as when I wake up on the first snow day of the year. I want it to last forever.

After a while, the voices grow softer. We're spread farther apart. Horses snort and sneeze. They whinny secrets back and forth.

Cassie and Rashawn fall back so I'm between them again.

"Where's Larissa?" Cassie asks.

I feel like somebody popped the bubble I've been floating in. "You had to ask."

"What?" Cassie sounds concerned. "What did I say?"

"Nothing."

"Tell us, Ellie," Rashawn urges. "What's up?"

So I tell them about Larissa's blog and the scare it gave me.

"You must have gone crazy!" Cassie exclaims.

"Really! You should have called us," Rashawn agrees.

That makes me feel good, that they'd want me to call them. I'm sure they call each other about everything. "Once we figured out it had to be Larissa writing the comments, I went from crazy to crazy mad."

They laugh. We ride without talking for a couple of minutes. Then Rashawn says, "So . . . so you're sure Larissa made the comment, right?"

I frown at her.

"I mean, did she admit she wrote that–about Dream being her horse?" Rashawn tugs her hair the way Miss Hernandez does when she's upset.

"Larissa wrote it, all right. She may not have admitted it. But come on. Who else would do a thing like that?" I ask.

Cassie laughs. "You have a point. I vote we forget about it."

"And I vote we forget about voting," Rashawn says. "It reminds me of our presidential blog. And it's much too beautiful out here to think about that now."

The rest of the ride is even better. Dream loves it as much as I do. It's like we're reading each other's mind. I start thinking how much fun it would be to trot. And the next thing I know, Dream breaks into a trot. When we go down a hill and it feels too fast, Dream slows down before I even signal her. And when we eat lunch, Dream enjoys her horse treats as much as I love Colt's peanut butter sandwiches.

On the ride back, Colt still hangs with the guys. But he manages to pull Bullet in front of me and Dream. And now and then he loops his reins around the saddle horn, sticks his hands behind his back, and signs something. *Did you see that hawk?* Or *How's Dream holding up?* Or *Want another sandwich?*

When we get back to the Harpers' stable, I can't believe we've been gone for over four hours. I'd happily turn around and do it all again.

Instead, Mr. Harper invites us to stay for some classic old horse movies. While we watch *National Velvet* and *The Black Stallion*, Mrs. Harper brings out so much food we can't even eat it all.

By the time Colt and I head home, the sun is setting. I'm thinking it's been a perfect day, even better than I imagined. As we ride up the dirt road toward our houses, I relive every detail of the day. Without words, I tell God how thankful I am for all of it. Who wouldn't be? A day like this. Friends like these. And a horse like Dream.

The road turns to gravel, and I know my house is just ahead. But the sun is so low it's hard to see.

"Hey! What's that about?" Colt asks. He stands in his stirrups and shields his eyes. "You expecting company?"

"Not that I know of." I tilt my head and try to see what he's talking about. A strange car is parked in front of my house. "Whose car is it?"

"I don't recognize it. It's a cool old car, though. It doesn't look like it's from around here."

We're almost to my house when the front door flies open. Out comes a boy I've never seen before. He stomps over to the road and points right at me. "There! Is she the one? Is she the one who stole my horse?"

7

Prove It

"What did you say?" Colt demands. He rides Bullet forward, placing himself between me and the tall, gangly boy with slicked-back black hair.

"You heard me," the boy says. "I want to know if she's the one who stole my horse." He points at me again. "She obviously is. I'd know my horse anywhere."

"You're crazy!" Colt snaps.

I should be jumping in here, but I can't. My

head is forming words, but my mouth can't get them out.

My dad steps out of the house. I expect him to agree with Colt, to kick this stranger out of our yard. "Let's all be calm here. Colt, you need to go home now."

This isn't making any sense. "Wh-why, Dad?"

"Please," Dad says.

Colt glances back at me. I don't want him to leave. He frowns from my dad to the boy to me. Then he signs, *Call me.* And he gallops away on Bullet.

I want to gallop after them.

Mom comes out of the house. Behind her is some woman I've never met. She's a head shorter than my mother but about twice as big around. Her light-blonde hair is wound on top of her head like a snake ready to strike. "Grayson," she says, "I told you to stay out of this."

"Why should I?" he fires back. "It's my horse, Aunt Deb!"

My fingers grip Dream's reins tighter. "This is my horse."

"Oh yeah?" the boy shouts. "That's Jinx, and I can prove it!"

"Jinx?" At this point I know he's crazy.

His aunt steps up behind him. Now I can see that there's another person behind her. A tall, thin girl with strawberry-blonde hair and blue eyes. She's younger than I am–maybe Ethan's age. She looks like a lost ballerina.

"Ellie," Mom says, "this is Mrs. Ford and her daughter, Annika. And Grayson, Annika's cousin. He's staying the summer with them in Cameron." Cameron is a little town a few miles down Highway 36.

Without so much as a glance at the strangers, I ask Mom, "Why are they here?"

"Ellie, honey," Mom begins, "put Dream away and meet us inside. We need to talk."

I turn away from them and walk Dream off toward the backyard. I don't want to talk.

When I get to the gate, Ethan opens it for me. I slide off Dream and sign, *What do you know about this, Ethan?*

He signs back, *They got here an hour ago. I missed most of it because nobody is signing. From what I can tell, the boy keeps saying Dream is his horse. I think he saw pictures on Larissa's blog.*

Larissa. I should have known.

I take my time brushing *my* horse. Ethan helps me. When I'm finished, I kiss Dream good night. There's nothing left to do but go in.

Annika and her mother are seated with Mom on the couch. Dad and that boy, Grayson, are sitting in the recliners. When I walk in, the room goes silent.

"Took you long enough," Grayson mutters.

"Grayson," his aunt says, "if you can't be civil, you can wait in the car."

"Good idea," I mutter back.

The woman turns to my mom. "Would you like to explain?" she asks.

Mom nods, then gets up and starts pacing. She circles the couch, her purple peasant skirt flowing behind her. "I don't have any idea how to explain. This whole thing makes about as much sense as hot sauce in a berry pie."

Mrs. Ford turns to me. "I'm so sorry about this, Ellie. It's easy to see you've taken great care of that horse. We saw the before and after pictures on that girl's website."

"There was an after picture on Larissa's blog?" The only picture I saw of Dream was the scraggly one.

"The pinto was in the background," Annika

explains, so softly I can barely hear her. "Larissa was getting a trophy. But the pinto outside the ring looked great." She glances at her cousin. "When Grayson saw how good the horse looks now, that's when he wanted to find her."

"That's not true!" Grayson protests.

I sign to Ethan as fast as I can, trying to fill him in.

"Like I said, my nephew is visiting us for the summer," Mrs. Ford continues. "A friend of Annika's was over, and she showed us the blog. She and Larissa go to the same horse shows. When Grayson saw the photos, he started screaming that it was his horse. He called his father, and Martin asked me to check things out. Annika's friend contacted Larissa, and that's how we ended up here. I wasn't even sure it was the same horse. But I knew we'd never hear the end of it if we didn't at least check it out."

"It's the same horse, all right," Grayson insists. "You've got Jinx, and I want her back."

"Grayson?" Mrs. Ford sighs.

Ethan steps in and signs to Dad. *Even if it's the same horse, they gave the horse away. They can't change their minds now, can they?*

Dad turns to Mrs. Ford and repeats Ethan's question.

"We didn't give Jinx away!" Grayson shouts. "We thought she ran away. She was always jumping the stable fence. The last time she did it, we were on vacation. Nobody told us. By the time we got back, we couldn't find her. It wasn't *our* fault. We thought she'd run off for good." He glares at me. "Only now we know the truth. You stole my horse!"

"She is *not* your horse!" I shout back.

"Believe me," Mrs. Ford says. "I don't like this whole business any more than you do. Maybe the first thing to do would be to identify the horse."

"How do you propose to do that?" Dad asks, his voice sharp as tacks.

"Well," she continues, "Grayson's father says their pinto had black-and-white spots."

"A lot of horses do," I snap.

"Do a lot of horses have one big spot that looks like a saddle?" Grayson demands. "Jinx does."

I can't answer. I feel like I've been kicked in the stomach by a wild horse. My favorite spot. Dream's biggest spot. It's shaped like a shiny black saddle.

8

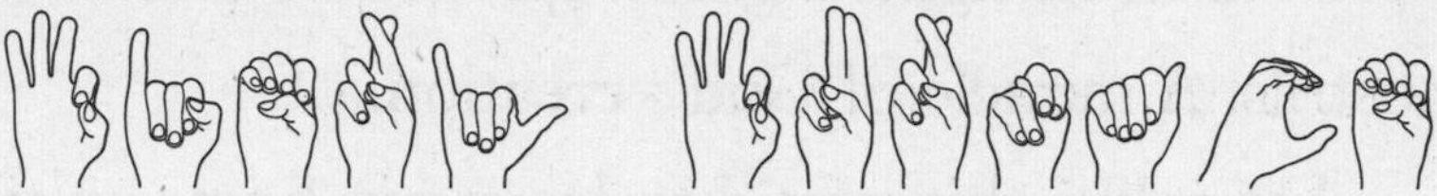

Fiery Furnace

Sunday morning when I wake up, my head hurts. I know I've had a horrible nightmare. Only I can't remember it.

Then I do remember. The worst nightmare I've ever had . . . and it was real.

Someone wants to take away my Dream.

Panic stabs both sides of my head. I rush to my window, open it, and scream, "Dream! Dream! Dream!"

Dream gallops to my window. She sticks her

head inside. I sit on the window ledge and run my fingers down her blaze. I memorize this jagged streak of white lightning that spreads down to her nostrils. A miracle of God's creation.

I stay like this, afraid to leave my horse, until Mom hollers that I have to get ready for church.

I can't eat, so I just pick at my scrambled eggs until they look like my brain feels. After a few minutes, Mom tells me to get dressed.

I pull clothes from my closet and put them on. But if somebody were to ask me what I'm wearing, I'd have no idea.

A horn honks. Suddenly I realize the house feels really quiet. Everybody else must be in the car already. I take one more long look out the window to make sure Dream is still there. Then I drag myself to the car and climb into the backseat.

"Where's Ethan?" Dad asks. He signs it too, as if Ethan were here to sign back.

I shrug.

"That boy's never late," Mom says. "He's probably worried about that little fish that's looking so poorly." She squints out the back window. "There he is. I think he's coming from Colt's house."

In a minute Ethan hops in. *Sorry. I was talking to Colt.*

Nobody says anything. We all know what they were talking about.

Our car has never been so quiet. I stare out the window on the way to church and imagine I'm riding Dream. Dream and I have ridden every road in Hamilton. I picture us galloping now, keeping pace with the car. I imagine jumping ditches and hedges as we pass by.

I close my eyes. I don't want to imagine anything else.

Dad parks the car, and I follow Ethan into church. We take the front right pew because that's where the interpreter, Mrs. Gorton, stands. Mrs. Gorton has white hair and could play Mrs. Santa Claus without a costume. She signs all the songs, the announcements, and the sermon. Sometimes I watch her to see what she leaves out so I can tell Ethan later.

Only not today. This morning I'm not watching or listening. My head feels like it's underwater—so deep nobody can get to me. I stand up and sit down when Ethan does. But I don't sing. Ethan sways to the music even though he can't hear it. He says he can feel the organ vibrate. And I guess he can, because he's always right with the rhythm. His fingers move through the lyrics, signing the words, and I know he's singing in his heart.

But I'm not.

I don't hear a word of the sermon until halfway through, when Ethan elbows me.

Don't you wish Colt were here? he signs.

I frown at him and shrug. Then I hear Pastor Alan say, "They refused to worship Nebuchadnezzar, even when he threatened to throw them into the fiery furnace." I figure he must be talking about Shadrach, Meshach, and Abednego.

"They told the king that they knew God could save them from getting burned to death. But even if God didn't come to their rescue, they'd still be okay. They could get through anything because God would be with them. And when old Nebuchadnezzar peeked into that fiery furnace, he saw four people walking around. Our three friends had the Lord with them, even in the middle of the fire."

Our pastor keeps going with the story, but I can't hear him. I'm too busy imagining Grayson in a crown, about to push Dream and me into a fiery furnace.

When we get home from church, Ethan races into the house. Munch barks and chases after him.

Squash runs after him too. When the rest of us trail in, my brother is standing over the fish tank. He turns around, and his face says it all. *Abednego,* he signs. *He's dead.*

We hover over Ethan and his dead fish.

"I'm sorry, Son," Dad says. He pats Ethan on the head.

"It's all my fault," Mom insists. "I never should have brought you an almost-dead fish. I hope you know that you got more life out of that little guy than anyone else could have."

"I'm sorry, Ethan," I say, signing it at the same time. I want to come up with something more. I just can't think of anything to say. He looks so sad, as if he's known this fish his whole life.

Ethan chooses a "burial at sea" for his fish. The four of us gather around the toilet. Ethan holds Abednego by the tail. He closes his eyes, and Mom and Dad do too.

I know my brother is praying. I wish he'd sign it. I want to know what he and God are talking about. Because somehow when Ethan prays, things happen.

Ethan opens his eyes and smiles. Then he flushes the toilet. *He was a good fish,* Ethan signs. *I'd better go check on Shadrach and Meshach.*

☆ ☆ ☆

The rest of the day I spend with Dream. We walk, trot, and canter all over Hamilton . . . as if this will be our last ride.

It's getting dark when we arrive back home. Just as I get to the house, Mom drives up with Dad and Ethan in the car. I realize I've missed our Sunday evening supper out at Crazy Larry's Dairies. But I don't care. I wouldn't have wanted to leave my horse.

I brush Dream and get her settled, then walk inside.

There's a voice I don't recognize, and at first I think there's someone else in the house. But when I tiptoe to the kitchen, I only see Mom and Dad and Ethan. They're huddled over the phone. The voice I hear is coming from the answering machine. Dad hits the button again, and I listen as Mom signs to Ethan.

"This is Martin Clayton, Grayson's father. I know my sister brought the kids to your house and confirmed that you have our horse. We would prefer not to involve the authorities. My sister believes you came upon the horse by accident. Apparently she was unable to resolve this herself. I'll be in your area tomorrow. I'll make arrangements to haul the horse away at your convenience. Please call me when you get this message."

His voice sounds like a television announcer's.

I picture a larger version of Grayson. The man gives his phone number and again asks–no, *tells*– us to call him back. He ends the call with something like "The law is the law, and it's on our side."

The machine clicks off. All eyes turn to me.

Without a word, I walk to my room, fall onto my bed, and cry myself to sleep.

9

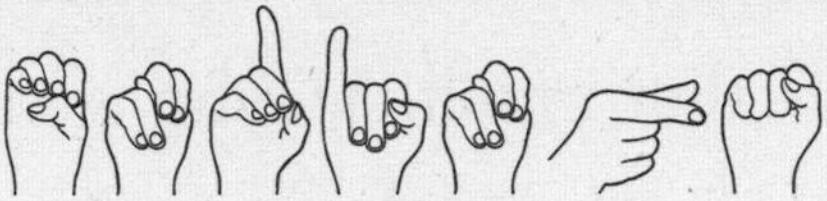

Endings

Monday is our last day of school. Ethan and I always celebrate the end of school with a crazy breakfast. Mom lets us choose chocolate cake, hot fudge sundaes, ice cream cones, or anything else we dream up.

But this morning neither of us is hungry. I sit at the breakfast table and listen to my dad's report on how he and Mom have tried everything they could think of to keep Dream. I stare into my orange juice and nod like I'm taking in Dad's explanations. Only I feel like I'm asleep. I'm still in the middle of my nightmare. I want to wake up and discover that none of this is really happening.

"I'm being honest with you, honey," Dad says. "You deserve that much. Maybe we should have done something more when we first got Dream. Maybe we could have legally claimed your horse then. I just don't know."

"This is nobody's fault," Mom says. She hasn't stopped pacing. She's still in her fuzzy, rainbow-colored bathrobe. Green slippers peek out like little nightmare monsters hiding under the bed skirt. "We were on the phone half the night with our lawyer. She says there was nothing we could have done then." Mom stops pacing. "And there's nothing we can do now."

I swallow hard. "When . . . wh-when will . . . ?" I can't go on.

Ethan finishes my question: *When will they come for Dream?*

Mom and Dad exchange a look that says it all. Then Dad answers, "Grayson and his father are coming this evening."

I get up from the table.

Mom swoops beside me. "I had a good conversation with Mrs. Ford. She said they'll keep Dream for the summer while Grayson is staying with them. She said Annika made a special point to invite you to visit whenever you want."

I nod. But I know I won't visit. How could I? How could I stand seeing Dream–*Jinx*–and then leaving her again?

Mom drives Ethan and me to school. I stare at my old tennis shoes. I can't bear looking out the window at the places Dream and I have ridden. The places we'll never ride again.

Ethan elbows me. *I'm still praying it won't happen,* he signs.

Me too, I sign back. And it's true. I haven't stopped

praying for a miracle. Every time I woke up in the night, I asked God to keep Grayson and his father far away from my horse. *But what if God says no?* I sign to Ethan without saying it aloud like we usually do. *What if God lets them take Dream away from me?*

Ethan doesn't look away. *It will be okay. You will be okay, Ellie. You'll see.*

I want more. I want Ethan to promise me that God won't let this nightmare come true. I want him to promise that something will happen to let me keep my horse. But I know he can't promise me that. Nobody can.

☆ ☆ ☆

"Ellie!" Cassie runs up to our car as soon as my mom pulls into the loading zone.

Rashawn is right behind her. "Colt told us everything. I can't believe this is happening!"

They hug me and keep their arms around me as we walk inside. I can tell Cassie has been crying. It makes me cry too.

"Th-they're coming tonight," I manage to get out. "They're taking Dream away. I don't know what I'll do–" I can't finish because I'm crying too hard.

"I talked to my aunt," Rashawn says. "She's a lawyer in Kansas City. But she doesn't know anything we can do either. It's so unfair!"

When we reach our classroom, Ashley and three of her friends come up to me.

"We think it's horrible, Ellie!" Ashley says. "I wish I could do something to help. I just can't believe what Larissa did to you!"

"Yeah. That's pretty low," Hunter agrees. Hunter Van Slyke is one of Larissa's best friends. At least I thought she was.

I look up through the mob of girls circled

around me, and I see Larissa. She's already in her seat, staring at her desk.

I sit down. Dylan and a couple of Colt's other buddies stop by and tell me they're sorry about my horse.

I don't know what to say to anybody.

When we're all at our desks, Colt signs to me, *I'll walk you home. We can run away if you want.*

I sign, *Thanks.* Part of me wants to say yes to running away with Dream and Colt and Bullet. But what good would that do? They'd come after us and take Dream anyway. I have to think of Dream now. I have to make this as easy as I can on her.

Miss Hernandez has us finish our blog presentations. Nobody is into it. Ashley and Rashawn report on their presidential blog. But Ashley starts tearing up when Rashawn tells about one candidate who owns horses. So they cut it short and sit down.

At recess everybody in our class–except Larissa–flocks around me.

"I think I'd take my horse and run away as far as I could if anybody ever tried to take Misty," Cassie says.

"I thought about it." I glance at Colt. "But they'd just find us. And they might take it out on Dream. I have to help my horse get through this. I'm hoping I can still call them sometimes to make sure they're taking good care of her."

"They sure didn't take good care of her before." Rashawn reties the red bow on her braid. "What did they have to say about that?"

"Yeah!" Dylan agrees. "We all saw what your horse looked like before you started taking care of her."

I tell them what Grayson said about Dream getting loose while they were gone and only getting skinny after she'd run away.

"I'll bet," Hunter says.

"My dad made Grayson's dad e-mail photos of Dream and Grayson together," I explain. "He wanted to make sure they really did own her first. They sent us a dozen pictures. Dream looked healthy in all of them. I guess she got scrawny when she was on her own. Or when she got bounced between rescues."

"I still don't get it," Colt says. I'm sitting on one of the swings, and he's standing on the other one. He's not swinging, just twisting and untwisting. "How could they lose a horse, for crying out loud? They must not have wanted to find her that badly. If I lost Bullet, I'd never stop looking for him."

"And what about the stable where she was staying? Why didn't they keep looking for her?" Cassie asks, like she can't believe it either.

I twist my swing like Colt's doing. "I guess somebody thought Grayson took Dream–only they called her Jinx. Nobody at the stable could believe she'd jumped their fence."

"Some stable," Dylan mutters.

"Some jumper," Colt says. He sounds proud of that fact.

We exchange looks. I know we're both remembering how Dream jumped the fence in my backyard. Dad had to build the fence higher to keep her in. But at least when Dream jumped our fence, she came right back home.

"And some name. Jinx is a rotten thing to call any horse," Colt says.

"No wonder she ran away," Dylan chimes in.

"Where do you think she was all that time?" Rashawn asks.

It's a question I've asked myself a hundred times. "Nobody knows for sure. She went to at least two rescues we know of. Still, nobody will ever know where Dream was when she was missing."

"And nobody would have ever known she was here if it hadn't been for *Starring Larissa*!" Colt says.

We all turn and stare at Larissa. Her eyes grow big. Then she looks away and walks into the school building, her nose in the air.

10

Good-Bye

Colt keeps his word and walks me home, even though Dylan tries to get him to go to baseball practice. "Ellie, listen to me!" Colt says. "If you don't want to run away, I have another idea."

"What?" I try to hope. I want Colt to have a real plan. I want God to pull off a real miracle.

"We let them take Dream. Then we break into their barn or pasture and take her back."

I sigh. "And they'll never guess who did it, right?"

"Maybe they'll quit looking like they did last time?" Colt doesn't sound so sure of himself.

"How are we supposed to get to Cameron in the first place? If we do get there, how are we going to get Dream back? And if we do get her back, then what? What do we do when they come looking for her? And what do you think my parents would do if–?"

"Okay, okay." Colt kicks an invisible ball. Hard. "I didn't say the plan was perfect."

"I know. Thanks for trying. At least you had a plan. Everything still feels like a nightmare. I can't stop hoping I'll wake up. Now that's a lousy plan."

We turn onto our road, and Colt stops dead. "Man, they're not wasting any time, are they?"

A black horse trailer is parked in front of my house. I freeze. Everything goes blurry. I can hear Colt's voice, but it sounds far away.

Ethan runs up to us. His fingers are moving so fast I can't read them.

"Slow down, Ethan," Colt says.

Ethan signs again. *They were here when I got home. Dad told Mr. Clayton he had to wait until you got here. Then Mom got home from the reptile rescue.*

"What did *she* tell him?" Colt asks.

She told him to hold his horses, Ethan signs.

Ethan and Colt fall in on either side of me. We bump arms as we walk toward the ugly black trailer. Our footsteps echo like thunder in my ears. I stretch on my tiptoes to see if I can spot Dream inside the trailer. It looks like a prison, with bars on the side windows. But I'm too short to see anything. And tears are blurring what I do see.

"Ellie!" Dad calls. "You made it!"

Mom is planted firmly next to him. "When I found out what was going on, I was ready to lie down in front of that trailer."

"She'd do it too!" Colt shouts.

I turn to see who Colt's shouting to.

Annika comes walking up from the side of the house. I think she's crying. "I'm so sorry, Ellie. I told Grayson and Uncle Martin to wait. But they thought they'd be doing you a favor by taking the horse before you got home."

"Where are they?" I ask, my voice shaking.

Annika motions to the backyard. "They can't catch her."

I push past all of them until I'm at the gate. Grayson and his dad are running at opposite ends of the yard. They're trying to corral Dream. It makes me think of the day I saw Dream galloping across the school yard with animal control chasing after her. They didn't have any luck either.

Suddenly I'm aware that Annika is beside me. "Please tell them to stop chasing her," I beg. "I'll catch my horse."

Annika climbs to the top of the fence and shouts, "Grayson! Uncle Martin! Come over here!"

Her uncle and cousin look shocked. Maybe they've never heard her yell before. They run over to the gate.

"That horse is crazy!" Grayson says.

His father is panting. Sweat streaks his white shirt. "Is it always this hard to catch?"

I ignore them and slip through the gate. I take a few steps into the yard and call, "Dream!"

That's all it takes. She trots up to me. She snorts, then nods as if agreeing with me. I throw my arms around her neck. I feel like a traitor as she follows me back toward the gate. I want to give Grayson and his dad a lesson in how to catch a horse. Don't walk or run straight at her. Don't look her in the eyes. Act like you know she wants to see you. Love her.

But even if I could say all this without crying, they wouldn't listen.

Grayson tosses me a lead rope. Once I snap it

to Dream's halter, he jogs over to us. "I can take it from here."

It's not easy, but I step aside.

Grayson stands to Dream's left and faces forward. He folds the excess rope the way he should, not wrapping it around his hand. Somebody has at least taught him something about horses.

"Grayson's had two years of riding lessons at the stable in Kansas City," his father says.

I turn to look at him. "K. C. Stables?"

"Right," he answers. "How did you know?"

I shrug. I knew because that's where Larissa keeps her horse, Custer's Darling Delight. Is that where Dream will have to live after the summer's over? I can't even think about it.

Dream lets Grayson lead her around the side of the house. They get as far as the trailer before my horse puts on the brakes.

Grayson turns and frowns at her. "Come on. We're almost there."

Dream stiffens her forelegs, locking her knees and digging in. She refuses to go another step.

"She won't go in, Dad," Grayson whines. "I can't load her."

"Here, I'll do it." Mr. Clayton takes the lead rope. He walks Dream in a big circle. As she passes by me, she turns her head and stares at me. I can almost hear my horse ask me, *Why?*

Warm tears choke my throat and make me cough.

The trailer's ramp is down. Dream lets Mr. Clayton lead her right up to the back of the trailer. But my horse refuses to set foot on the ramp.

"Has this horse ever ridden in a trailer?" Mr. Clayton demands.

"Yes." I walk up and take the rope. "Please step back."

When he doesn't back off, Annika shouts, "Uncle, just get out of the way!"

As soon as Mr. Clayton is out of our sight, I walk straight up the ramp and into the left side of the trailer. Dream follows me. "Good girl, Dream," I murmur, stroking her soft forehead and her beautiful blaze.

I'm standing with her when Grayson storms up the other trailer stall. He takes the rope out of my hands. "*I'll* tie her. You better go now."

I run my hand over Dream as I back out of the dark and musty trailer.

A minute later Grayson jumps down from the trailer, causing it to shake. Then his dad slams the tailgate shut, closing in my Dream.

11

Not Again

I stare at the back of the trailer, at the closed tailgate.

The pickup pulling the trailer fires up its engine. Exhaust puffs from the tailpipe.

Annika sticks her head out the window and hollers, "Ellie! I mean it! We'll have Dream all summer. You can come and visit her whenever you want!"

"Thank you," I mutter. But one good-bye is one too many. I couldn't go through this again.

The pickup rolls forward. The trailer jerks behind it. I walk alongside the trailer, keeping pace as long as I can. "She loves apples!" I call after them. "And she hates being cooped up in a stall. Let her graze. And she loves treats! Go to Winnie the Horse Gentler's website for recipes!"

Only it's too late. They can't hear me.

I watch as the trailer fades into a cloud of dust. That trailer is taking away one of the most important things in my life. Dream. *My* Dream.

Couldn't You have stopped them? I ask God.

I can sense God watching with me, just looking on as my horse disappears. I think about Abednego, Ethan's dead fish. About the real Shadrach, Meshach, and Abednego. God could have kept all of them far from danger. I know that. *Ethan is okay in spite of his dead fish,* I tell God. *My brother knows You well enough to still be okay, even though You didn't save his fish. But I'm not like Ethan, God. I don't feel okay. I don't get it. And I don't know how I'm going to make it without Dream.*

I'm not sure how much time passes while I'm standing by the side of the road. Pinto Cat finds me. As if she knows what's going on, she stares down the road with me. We watch the spot where the trailer disappeared. I'm sort of aware when Ethan and Colt wander off to ball practice and Mom and Dad go inside.

Finally I turn and head back to the house. I'm almost to our front door when I hear something. On the road behind me I'm sure I hear pounding horse's hooves. Trotting. Then cantering. If I didn't know better, I'd think . . .

Then she nickers.

I spin around, knowing it's Dream. "Dream!" I take off, running as fast as I can.

We meet in the middle of the road. Dream rears and tosses her mane. She's sweating like she's been galloping. I hug her. I cry. What's happening? I don't understand.

Clang! Bang! The empty trailer–that monster–wheels around the corner.

Dad comes out of the house. "Ellie, what's going on? Where did–?"

"Well, I'll be a monkey's mama!" Mom says, running behind him.

The trailer pulls up. All three of them get out.

"I told you so, Grayson," his dad says.

"It wasn't my fault!" Grayson whines.

"Really?" his dad challenges.

"Really!" Grayson insists. "All I wanted to do was see why that rope came untied. How was I supposed to know the stupid horse would back out of the trailer when I wasn't looking? And so what? We have her again. Big deal!"

Annika scooches in front of her uncle and gets nose to nose with her cousin. "It *is* a big deal, Grayson! If we hadn't taken the back roads, Dream might have run into traffic. She could have been hurt! And now look what you've done. Ellie has to say good-bye to her horse all over again."

"*My* horse!" Grayson shouts. "And her name is Jinx, not Dream. If Ellie had done a better job training *Jinx*, none of this–"

My mom makes a noise that's somewhere between a growl and a snort. She walks up to Grayson. Towering over him, she says, "Young fella, I have a word of advice for you from my own mama: 'Never miss a good chance to keep your trap shut.'"

Grayson's mouth snaps closed.

"Come on, Dream," I whisper. She follows me into the trailer. I take my time tying one of the knots Ethan taught me. "There. Now you be good. Do what they say, hear?" I press my cheek next to hers. And I kiss her good-bye for what I'm sure will be the last time.

12

Can't

For the next couple of weeks, I can't eat. I can't sleep. I can't stop crying. I can't be nice to anybody. I can't play ball with Ethan or make up rhymes with Dad. When Mom drags me to the cat farm with her, I can't even pet the stray cats. They run away from me.

At night I still ask God to bless everybody. But God feels far away. So does my family. I'm living in the same house with them, but it's like I'm on the other side of the universe. Alone.

Every morning the first thing I do when I wake up is open my window and wait for Dream. But of course she doesn't come. I know she won't. She can't. Yet I can't stop opening the window for her.

Annika calls us almost every day to tell us how Dream is doing. I can't bear to talk to her. But sometimes when she's on the line with my parents, I listen on the extension. Once she described to Mom how she went to Winnie the Horse Gentler's website and copied a recipe for a horse treat with apples and molasses. She made it and gave it to Dream. Dream loved it. Annika even calls Dream "Dream"–at least in her phone calls.

Another time Annika leaves a message on the answering machine: "You really should come and watch Grayson try to catch Dream, Ellie. It's pretty funny. That pinto is so smart–a lot smarter than my cousin. And when Grayson does get Dream and saddles her for a ride, it's even funnier. He can't get

Dream to do anything he wants. He's gotten her to walk a couple of times. But she won't trot or canter for him. And don't worry. Mom told Grayson he's not allowed to use spurs or a whip or a quirt or anything. So he usually gives up pretty quick."

Colt calls every day and asks me to come over and ride Bullet. He pleads with me to help him work on barrel racing. Sometimes he calls to see if I want to ride double and go on a breakfast ride, like we used to do with Bullet and Dream.

Only there's no way. It would hurt too much to do those things without Dream.

One Saturday Colt shows up at my house before I'm even out of bed. He almost begs me to go to horsemanship practice with him. Cassie and Rashawn both called me the night before. Even Mr. Harper got in on it. He called and talked to Mom, trying to get her to make me go to practice.

But I can't do that. I can't do anything.

☆ ☆ ☆

On my third Friday night without Dream, I can't sleep. I lie in bed but kick off my covers. The moon shines through my window, right where Dream used to stick her head in.

Finally I climb out of bed and walk to the window. I stare out at the too-tall grass. Dream kept our yard in good shape. The grass never got too long.

I sit on my windowsill, then swing my legs over and jump down. It's not much of a jump. Pinto Cat trots up and rubs against my legs. She purrs, then goes back to the lean-to. She misses Dream too.

I stroll through the backyard, where I can still smell Dream. There's not a thing I can do to get her back . . . except pray.

God, I can't do this. I can't stop hurting. I can't do anything to end this nightmare.

But I know You can. You could have stopped this from happening. You could have kept Grayson from seeing Larissa's blog. You could have kept them from coming to claim Dream. You could have made them leave my horse alone. You could have let Dream stay right here. With me, where she belongs. Instead, You let them take her away.

I've wandered deep into my backyard. When Dream was here, this was my favorite spot in the whole world. Now the yard feels empty. And I feel alone.

Only I'm not alone. I know Mom and Dad are a shout away. Ethan is as close as a wave of my hand.

But there's more to it than that.

In my heart, I silently tell God, *I know You're here. After everything else is gone, You'll still be here–so close I don't even have to say words out loud.*

I gaze up at the half-moon surrounded by

blinking stars. It looks like they're speaking sign language. Or star language. And I'm grateful that my God really isn't far away someplace, beyond the moon and the stars. *You're here. You're inside of me. You're closer than close.*

And I think maybe that's the secret. Maybe that's what Shadrach, Meshach, Abednego, and Ethan all knew. Whatever happens, we'll be okay because God will be there. No matter what goes away, God won't. And even if I cry myself to sleep every night for the rest of my life, I won't be by myself. God will be there with me–if I'm in my bed, in a fiery furnace, or in an empty backyard.

13

Okay

Saturday morning I open the window to my bedroom and let in the morning chill. My first thought is *I miss you, Dream.* But my second is *Morning, Lord. How about we go for a ride?*

When I walk into the dining room, Dad is already sharing his "office" with Mom and Ethan.

"Donuts," Dad says, pointing to an almost-empty box at the end of the table.

I take the powdery one. "Thanks. You guys are up early."

"Rhymes," Dad says, not looking up from his

laptop. "And jingles." His hair is nicely combed, so he must be doing fine on his own.

"It's the Doggone Drive," Mom explains. "Thought I bit off more than I could chew. But it turns out my mouth is bigger than I realized. We're chewing just fine. Drive on, little doggies!"

Ethan grins at me. *We found Lucky. Some kid recognized the dog from the picture on the dog food cans. The owners were so grateful that they called the TV station to make a public thank-you.*

Dad finishes the good news. "And your mother is going to be on television. Noon edition."

"Wow! That's great, Mom!"

Mom laughs. "And won't they be surprised when I walk onstage! They actually told me to wear solid colors–black or navy."

"They do not know your mother," Dad observes.

"Pull up a sit-down, Ellie." Mom taps the chair next to her. "The Doggone Drive marches on."

Ethan waves a picture of a Chihuahua at me. They already have half a dozen cans of dog food with the little dog's picture pasted on them.

"I'll help later, okay?" I say.

"Going somewhere?" Dad asks.

"Horsemanship practice," I answer.

All three heads snap toward me like I've just announced I'm going to Paris.

"Well, if that's not the cat's pj's!" Mom exclaims.

"If wishes were fishes," Dad begins, "then . . . hmmm . . . wishes, fishes . . ." He scribbles furiously on his yellow pad. Then he starts pounding his laptop keys.

Good for you, Sis, Ethan signs.

"Okay," I say and sign. "Better hurry if I want to catch a ride with Bullet and Colt."

I can hear their group sigh of relief as I leave the room.

☆ ☆ ☆

"It's about time," Colt says when I show up in his barn.

"Yep," I agree.

Colt mounts Bullet and helps me climb up behind him. The saddle slips a little, but not too much. Maybe Bullet is losing more weight.

Colt waits until I'm settled behind him to ask, "So are you okay?" I can't see Colt's face, but I can picture it. His eyes will be wide, and he'll be biting his bottom lip, worried about my answer.

"I'm okay," I tell him. "I just figured that out. I miss Dream like crazy, and I always will. But I'm okay, Colt."

"Yeah?" he asks. And I get the feeling he's also asking something else. Maybe it's because Colt and I have had so much practice "talking" without words when we sign, but I can read him. I'm pretty sure he's asking me how I can be okay without Dream. Like, what's the secret of being okay when you've lost what you love? Colt has lost a lot this year with the divorce.

"It's God, Colt," I answer. "I figure that since God is still here, I'll be okay. I am okay."

For a minute, he doesn't say anything. He doesn't move. We just sit there on Bullet. I breathe in the smell of hay and horse. Sunlight streaks through the open barn door and splashes my back, warming it. Above us, in the rafters, a dozen sparrows tweet.

"Okay, then," Colt says.

And we ride Bullet out into the bright sunshine.

14

Change

Cassie, Rashawn, and Ashley come galloping toward Colt and me as soon as we reach the fairgrounds.

"I knew you'd come!" Cassie cries. She's riding Misty bareback. Her feet dangle close to the tall grass as she and her pony thunder toward us.

Ashley trots up on Warrior, the Harpers' jumper. The gelding looks better every time I see him. "Ellie, you can ride any of our horses you want," she offers.

"Thanks, Ashley," I tell her.

"You should come over and ride Misty with me tomorrow," Cassie says.

"How about me?" Rashawn asks. "Come on, you guys. If any horse can handle riding double, it's Dusty." Rashawn laughs and strokes her giant horse's neck.

The rest of us laugh too. It feels good. I think we're all relieved to have something to laugh about.

"No way," Colt says. "If you think Bullet and I are giving Ellie a free ride here today, you've got another think coming. She owes me now. Ellie has to set up the barrels for Bullet. Then she's got to train both of us in barrel racing."

Jonathan and Aiden and a couple of the others greet me like they've really missed me at practice. Jonathan says it hasn't been the same without me, even though we've never said more than a couple of words to each other.

Only Larissa keeps her distance. She stays

at the far end of the arena by herself. Custer's Darling Delight looks beautiful–shiny and ready to show off.

Colt urges Bullet to the center of the arena. The other horses and riders move with us, keeping us in the middle of the herd.

It's great having friends who care this much. I'm grateful. I hope they know that.

I end up riding Spirit, one of the Harpers' horses. She's older, but she's in great shape. The mare still wins ribbons in palomino pleasure classes.

Ashley helps me saddle Spirit. She talks me into tacking her up English. It's only the second time I've tried riding with a four-rein bridle. "You can handle the bridle," Ashley insists. "I'm not worried, and neither is Spirit."

Ashley may be right about Spirit. The mare holds still while I mount. When I take the reins–

two in each hand–Spirit arches her neck and waits for me to cue her.

I like riding Spirit. Who wouldn't? But I ache for Dream. For three years I had to ride one of Mr. Harper's horses because I didn't have one of my own. Now here I am again.

But so are You. Right, God? You're here too. So we're okay.

"Walk out!" Mr. Harper calls from the center of the arena. "Space yourselves!"

We keep close to the arena's path. I hardly have to use the reins to guide Spirit. Right away I can tell she's used to the other aids–legs, weight, voice, and hands. I'm not as in tune with her as I was with Dream. Dream could read my mind. But Spirit makes it easy to ride English. She knows what she's doing.

"Teee-rot!" Mr. Harper calls out.

About half of us are riding English, so we post

to the trot. Instead of trying to keep our seats in the saddle like the Western riders, we rise out of the saddle every other stride. Up and down. Up and down. I used to have to count one, two, one, two. But now I can feel the rhythm. I don't even have to think about it. I know it's because I've ridden Dream bareback so much this year. Some horses have such a rough trot. Not Dream. Dream has a sweet, smooth trot.

"Relax those backs, Aiden and Isabella!" Mr. Harper shouts. "Gently now. Feel the bumps. No double bumping. Keep those lower legs still, Ashley!"

When Spirit and I pass in front of Mr. Harper, he says, "Ellie, that's excellent! Perfect saddle seat. I like those ankles and toes. Nice job."

I know he's probably saying those things to make me feel better. But maybe not. I feel like a better rider than I was . . . before Dream.

Mr. Harper takes us back to a walk. We reverse and trot again. Then walk. After that he calls for a canter. I try to focus on Spirit, but my imagination takes me to Dream. In my mind, Dream and I are cantering around the arena.

We're halfway through the practice hour when a car speeds onto the fairgrounds. Dust makes a cloud around the car so I can't even tell what color it is. The driver doesn't slow down until the car is all the way to the arena. Brakes squeal. Several of the horses shy away. Aiden almost falls off.

I recognize the car, then the driver. It's Mrs. Stevens, Colt's mother.

Mrs. Stevens, dressed in a navy business suit that would be perfect for the noon edition of the news, steps out of her car as if it's on fire. She slams the driver's door and storms up to the arena, high heels fighting with the tall grass. "Colt! Get home right this minute. Do you hear me?"

Most of the kids look away.

Mr. Harper walks over to her. "Can I help you?"

Mrs. Stevens ignores him. "I mean it, Colt! Now!"

Colt trots Bullet up to her.

I want to sign something to him, but he's not looking my way.

"I'll come home after horsemanship," he says.

"Now!" she screams. "You know good and well this is your father's weekend. He'll be here any minute. I told you. You're going to St. Louis." She turns her back on him and makes her way to the car.

"And I told you I'm staying here." Colt says this in a calm, nice voice, which is more than I can say for his mother.

"What did you say?" she shouts from her car window.

Colt guides Bullet out of the arena and over to

his mother's car. He rides up to the window and says something I can't hear.

Colt's mother explodes. So does Colt. They shout, but their words bang into each other, so I can't tell what they're saying. Finally Mrs. Stevens starts the engine and backs the car away from Bullet. She drives off faster than she came.

Without looking back at us, Colt lets out a "Yee-haw!" Then he gallops away on Bullet.

I want to go after him. To help. To do something.

Only now I know a secret. I know that sometimes all you can do is pray. And that's enough. That's plenty, in fact. Because even if I can't be with Colt now, God is.

God, please help Colt know You're there with him. Let him be okay.

15

Double

"Back to work, riders!" Mr. Harper calls. "Teee-rot!"

We finish our practice. But we're all unusually quiet. Even our horses seem to be worried about Colt and Bullet. Misty, Cassie's pony, balks and refuses to canter. Even easygoing Dusty proves to be a handful for Rashawn. The big horse keeps trying to exit the arena. Several of the kids leave early without bothering to give Mr. Harper an excuse.

I stick it out until the end of our horsemanship session. Then I cool Spirit down and brush her.

I don't want her to get a chill on the ride back to the Harpers' stable.

It's not until all Mr. Harper's horses have been loaded into the trailer that I realize I don't have a ride home. The other horses and riders have left the fairgrounds. Except Larissa. Her driver is here with the trailer, waiting to take Custer's Darling Delight back to K. C. Stables.

"You need a lift?" Mr. Harper double-checks the trailer hitch before climbing into his truck. Ashley is already snapping her seat belt next to him.

There's not much room in the truck for me. Plus, my house is in the opposite direction. I don't want Spirit and the other horses to have a longer ride home.

"I'm good, Mr. Harper. Thanks. And thanks again for letting me ride Spirit." I back away from the trailer.

Ashley leans in front of her dad. "Call me,

Ellie. We'll go riding. Or go to a movie or something. Okay?"

"Deal," I answer, knowing Ashley would rather go to a movie. And I'd rather ride.

I wave at them until they're out of sight. I'm not sure I realized what good friends Ashley and her dad are to me.

I could call Mom or Dad to come get me. Or I could walk.

I decide to walk home. I'm not in any hurry to get back. If I had Dream, we'd take off on a long ride together. I hope Grayson realizes what a great horse Dream is. And I hope he stops calling her Jinx.

I haven't gotten far when I hear horse's hooves coming up behind me. The steps are light and sharp. This horse is prancing. I turn around to see who could be following me.

No way. "Larissa?"

Custer is high-stepping, getting closer with each hoof beat. The poor horse's eyes are bulging, and his mouth is open. Slobber drips to the ground as his nostrils flare. This horse has probably never been out on a real road before.

"What are you doing riding on the street?" I ask Larissa. I don't think I've ever seen Larissa on a horse outside an arena.

"It's a free country," she answers.

"So where's Custer's trailer?" I glance behind her and see the trailer creeping across the fairgrounds, coming our way.

"I told my driver to follow me," Larissa says.

I move beside Custer so he won't run over me. The giant trailer, empty, is now inching up on us. "Why?"

"I–I thought you might need a ride home," she answers.

"That's okay," I say. "I'm good."

Larissa looks like she just lost the trophy at a horse show. "B-but I knew you rode here double on Bullet. Colt's gone. You could ride double with me."

"On Custer?"

"Yes."

I'm pretty sure Larissa Richland has never let anyone ride her horse, single or double.

She pats Custer's narrow rump behind her English saddle. "Please?" she whispers. Her eyes are red, and I think I see tears leaking out. "Ellie, I'm so sorry. I didn't know. I didn't mean for it to happen. I didn't want you to lose Dream. I know everybody thinks it's my fault. And they're right. But I'd never have blogged at all if I'd known you'd lose your horse. You have to believe me. I wish I'd never put up that story."

This is a Larissa I don't know. I'm not sure what to say to this Larissa.

"Ellie, I know how much you loved Dream. I love to ride. I love to show. But you loved your horse. I can tell the difference. And now because of me, you don't have her anymore."

"It's not really your fault. It just happened." The words come out before I have a chance to think about what I'm saying.

"How can you say that?" she asks. "Everybody else believes I did this on purpose."

I think about the way kids have been staying away from Larissa. I guess I've been focusing on myself so much I haven't given that much thought. I've blamed her too. "I'm sorry, Larissa."

"*You're* sorry? *I'm* sorry! I said it first!"

"Now that's the Larissa I know," I say, grinning.

Larissa almost laughs.

I stare at Custer's Darling Delight, then at Larissa. "So are you going to give me a hand up or not?" I ask.

She takes her foot out of the stirrup, and I put my foot in to climb up.

Once I'm on Custer's back, he seems even taller than he did from the ground. And bonier. Much bonier.

"You okay back there?" Larissa asks.

"I'm okay," I answer. I laugh on the inside because I've been saying that a lot lately. *I'm okay.*

We ride for a while without talking. Then Larissa says, "How are you making it, Ellie? Without Dream, I mean?"

"Do you really want to know?"

"I asked, didn't I?" she says.

So I tell her what I told Colt. "I guess I can stand losing anything–even Dream–as long as I still have God."

She turns onto my street. "But don't you miss Dream?" Larissa asks.

"I miss Dream so much it hurts," I admit.

"Sometimes I imagine that I see her. She'll put her head through my window so I can pet her. Or I imagine that she comes galloping up the road to me. It's so real in my mind, I almost feel like she's there. Her smell. The sound of her hooves. Her mane flying in the wind."

I stop because I'm imagining that scene right this minute, as real as I've ever imagined anything. "Like now, for instance. I can almost see my horse galloping toward me–"

"Ellie, me too!" Larissa cries. "That *is* Dream!"

16

Home

I blink, then blink again. She's still there. A gorgeous black-and-white pinto is galloping toward Larissa and me.

"Dream," I whisper, because all the breath has gone out of me.

Dream trots up to us, not stopping until her nose is so close I can feel the warmth of her breath.

The tiny hairs on my arms stand up. I smell my Dream. I see her. She nickers. She's real. Really real. And she's here.

Reaching down, I half expect her to disappear when I touch her. I stroke her lightning blaze. I scratch her jaw and watch as her eyes close with pleasure. "You're here, Dream. You came home to me."

"How could she?" Larissa asks. I almost forgot that Larissa is here, that I'm sitting on her horse. "You're not saying your horse came all the way here from Cameron, are you?" Larissa says. "By herself?" She glances around like she's looking for a trailer. But the only trailer in sight is Larissa's. And it's stopped at the corner.

Then I notice the car in my driveway. It's the same old car Colt and I saw when we returned home from our trail ride. It's Mrs. Ford's car—Annika's mother, Grayson's aunt.

I slide off Custer and manage to swing onto Dream's bare back. She's so sweaty that my jeans stick to her. I lean into her neck and hug her.

I inhale my Dream. Even if they take her from me right now, I'm grateful for this second with my horse.

Mom, Dad, and Ethan come running up. They surround Dream and me.

"Annika and her mother are here, honey," Mom says.

And Grayson, Ethan signs.

I know Dream will have to leave with them once more. And my heart will break all over again. But it still feels like a gift.

Grayson's aunt is talking to him as they make their way up the sidewalk and out to the road. Annika trails along a little behind. When they're close enough, I strain to hear what they're saying.

"I want you to think about this very hard, Grayson," Mrs. Ford says. "There's no going back from a thing like this, you hear? So tell me now: do you mean what you're saying?"

"Yes! I'll put it in writing if it makes you feel any better!" Grayson shouts. "I told you a hundred times on the way over here. And Dad says I can do whatever I want." Grayson kicks at the gravel and scowls at Dream and me. "I mean it!"

"You mean what?" I ask.

"I've had it with horses. Especially this one." Grayson points to Dream.

My mind races through all the ugly possibilities of what it will mean if Grayson rejects Dream. He might turn the horse over to his father. His father could sell Dream or ship her away forever. Or worse.

"Listen, Grayson," I begin. "Dream–*Jinx*–is a wonderful horse. You just have to get to know her . . . again. She's so willing to learn and full of love. She'll be a terrific friend if you let her. Maybe I could help. I probably should have gone to Cameron and helped you and Dream–Jinx–get used to each other. Give her another chance. Please!"

The whole time I'm pleading with him, Grayson scrunches up his face like he's eaten something rotten. He shakes his head. "No way. You can't teach an old dog new tricks."

"That doesn't make any sense," Larissa says. "This pinto is a horse, not a dog, in case you don't know the difference. And anyway, I've seen what Ellie can do with this horse."

I'm stunned. Larissa is sticking up for me. *And* Dream.

"I know a lot about horse shows," Larissa continues. "And that pinto could win ribbons for you. You should take Ellie up on her offer. She's fantastic with horses. Ellie could help you learn–"

"I don't want her help," Grayson snaps. "I'm done with this *backyard* horse. And that's final." He cocks his head toward his cousin, who hasn't said a word. "I'm giving this nag to Annika."

"Well, I'll be a lop-eared leprechaun," Mom mutters.

"Did the boy say he's giving the horse to his cousin?" Dad asks.

Mrs. Ford ignores Dad's question. She squats down and looks her nephew square in the eyes. "I'll ask you one more time, Grayson. Are you really giving this horse to Annika?"

"Yeah!" Grayson shouts. "How many times do I have to say it? Get the trailer and haul the beast to your house forever. Or better yet, Annika can ride it back to your house, for all I care. I'm going to wait in the car." He turns on his heels and stomps to their car, slamming the car door after him.

I feel as if I could cry and laugh at the same time. "Annika, I'm so happy for you. I know you'll be good to Dream. She'll be a great horse for you. And I promise she'll make a wonderful friend."

I scratch Dream's neck. "I'll help in any way I can. I can make you a list of Dream's favorite foods too. And I'll print out Winnie the Horse Gentler's recipes."

But Annika is shaking her head.

Suddenly I feel awkward. Maybe she thinks I'm trying to boss her around or something. She still hasn't said anything. I have no idea what she's thinking. Maybe she's not really interested in horses after all. Maybe she doesn't even want a horse.

"Look, Annika, I'm sorry. You don't have to make treats for Dream. I shouldn't have tried to tell you what to do."

"I don't want to give her treats," Annika says.

"Okay." I want to ask her why. Dream loves treats. Would it be such a big deal to make something your horse loves?

"That's not very nice," Larissa says. "Ellie

knows some great recipes for horse treats. The least you could do is–"

"I don't want to give Dream treats," Annika explains, "because Ellie should give her treats."

"I don't get it," I say.

"You should give Dream the treats because she's your horse," Annika says. "She always was. Grayson just didn't know it."

I stare at her. I can't speak. I'm afraid to say anything. Maybe I imagined what Annika said.

Annika's mother brushes a stray hair off her daughter's forehead. "Sweetheart, are you sure?"

"I've never been more sure of anything. Look at her, Mom. That horse belongs to Ellie. And Ellie belongs to her. This is Dream's real home." She grins at me. "Besides, we don't really have a backyard. And we all know Ellie's Dream is a backyard horse."

"All right!" Colt hollers.

I hadn't even noticed Colt and Bullet standing just across the road. Behind him I spot Colt's dad leaning against his fancy sports car.

How long have you been standing there? I sign to Colt.

Long enough, Colt answers. "Welcome home, Dream!"

Mom and Dad are falling all over themselves thanking Annika and her mother.

"Come on, Colt!" his dad shouts.

"I gotta go," Colt says. He looks from me to Ethan and back again. "So this must be one of those miracles you guys talk about, right?"

"Sure feels like one to me," I answer.

Colt nods and rides to his dad. Then, without turning back to us, he signs, *Thank you.* At least that's what I think he signs.

"Ethan?" I ask. "What was Colt thanking us for? Or did I get the sign wrong?"

Ethan's grin takes up half his face. *You got the sign right. But it wasn't for us, Ellie.*

I start to ask him what he means. But then I get it. Colt was thanking God.

Talk about miracles. . . .

Larissa and Custer's Darling Delight leave in the K. C. Stables trailer. Annika's mom drives off with Grayson and Annika after Annika promises to come and visit Dream and me this summer. Mom, Dad, and Ethan run to Crazy Larry's to pick up a cake to celebrate Dream's homecoming.

And that leaves Dream and me alone.

But not alone. Because if I've learned anything, I know this–I will never be alone again.

If we are thrown into the blazing furnace, the God whom we serve is able to save us. . . . But even if he doesn't . . . we will never serve your gods or worship the gold statue you have set up.

Daniel 3:17-18

Horse Talk!

Bay–A reddish-brown color for a horse. A bay horse usually has a black mane and tail.

Blaze–A facial marking on a horse (usually a wide, jagged white stripe).

Canter–A horse's slow gallop; a more controlled three-beat gait.

Cutting horse–A horse (usually a quarter horse) bred to separate cows from a herd. Some cutting horses also cut around barrels in barrel racing or compete in Western horse show classes and events.

English–A style of horseback riding that is often considered more formal and classic than Western style. Riders generally sit on a flat saddle, post (rise from the saddle) on a trot, and hold the reins in both hands.

Farrier–Someone trained to care for a horse's hooves. Farriers trim hooves and put shoes on horses, but many also treat leg and tendon problems.

Flanks–The indented part of a horse's body between the ribs and the hip. Flanks may be tender to the touch.

Foreleg–One of a horse's front legs.

Forelock–The piece of hair that falls onto a horse's forehead.

Gait–The way a horse moves, as in a walk, a trot, a canter, or a gallop.

Gallop–A horse's natural and fast running gait. It's speedier than a lope or a canter.

Gelding–A male horse that has had surgery so he can't mate and produce foals (baby horses). Geldings often make the calmest riding horses.

Habit–An outfit for horseback riding or showing, usually including some kind of tailored jacket and hat.

Halter–The basic headgear worn by a horse so the handler can lead the animal with a rope.

Hand–The unit for measuring a horse's height from the withers (area between the shoulders) to the ground. One hand equals four inches (about the width of an average cowboy's hand).

Hindquarters–The back end of a horse, where much of a horse's power comes from.

Hoof pick–A hooked tool, usually made of metal, for cleaning packed dirt, stones, and gunk from the underside of a horse's hoof.

Hunter–A horse that's bred to carry a rider over jumps. In a horse show, hunters are judged on jumping ability and style.

Lead rope–A length of rope with a metal snap that attaches to a horse's halter.

Lope–The Western term for *canter*. The lope is usually smooth and slower than the canter of a horse ridden English.

Mare–A female horse over the age of four, or any female horse that has given birth.

Muzzle–The soft portion of a horse's nose between the nostrils and the upper lip.

Nicker–A soft, friendly sound made by horses, usually to greet other horses or trusted humans.

Palomino–A horse that is cream or yellow-gold in color. Palominos may be found in a number of breeds, such as the quarter horse. Even backyard horses may be palominos.

Pinto–Any horse with patches or spots of white and another color, usually brown or black.

Post–To rise up and ease back down in the saddle when the horse is at a trot. This makes the gait more comfortable for the rider. English-style riders generally post at every step.

Quarter horse–An American horse breed named because it's the fastest horse for a quarter-mile distance. Quarter horses are strong and are often used for ranch work. They're good-natured and easygoing.

Quirt–A Western-style crop, or whip, with a short handle.

Saddle bags–Bags or pouches that balance across the back of a saddle and are used to carry supplies.

Saddle horse–A saddle horse could be any horse trained to ride with a saddle. More specifically, the American saddlebred horse is an elegant breed of horse used as three- and five-gaited riding horses.

Shetland pony–A small breed, no bigger than 10.2 hands, that comes from the Shetland Islands off Scotland. Shetland ponies are the ideal size for small children, but the breed is known to be stubborn and hard to handle.

Sorrel–A horse with a reddish-brown or reddish-gold coat.

Stallion–A male horse that hasn't had surgery to prevent him from mating and producing foals.

Swayback–A sagging back on a horse, or a horse with a deeply dipped back. Being swayback is often a sign of old age in a horse.

Three-gaited–Used to describe an American saddlebred horse that has been trained to perform at a walk, trot, and canter.

Throatlatch–The strap part of the bridle that helps keep the bridle on. It goes under a horse's throat, running from the right ear and loosely fastening below the left ear.

Trot–The two-beat gait where a horse's legs move in diagonal pairs. A trot is generally a choppy ride.

Western–A style of horseback riding used by cowboys in the American West. Western horseback riders usually use heavier saddles with saddle horns and hold both reins in one hand.

Whicker–A low sound made by a horse. A whicker is sometimes thought to be a cross between a whinny and a nicker.

Whinny–A horse's neigh, or to make a neighing sound. A whinny may be a horse's call to another horse or a cry of alarm.

Whorl–A twist of hair that grows in the opposite direction from the surrounding coat. This patch is usually on a horse's forehead.

Withers–The top of a horse's shoulders, between the back and the neck. The height of a horse is measured from the withers to the ground.

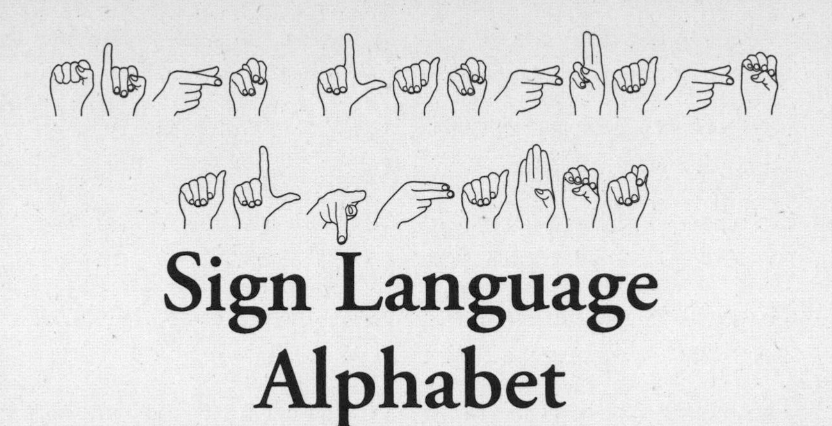

Sign Language Alphabet

A
B
C
D
E
F
G
H
I
J
K
L
M
N
O
P
Q
R
S
T
U
V
W
X
Y
Z

About the Author

Dandi Daley Mackall grew up riding horses, taking her first solo bareback ride when she was three. Her best friends were Sugar, a pinto; Misty, probably a Morgan; and Towaco, an Appaloosa. Dandi and her husband, Joe; daughters, Jen and Katy; and son, Dan (when forced), enjoy riding Cheyenne, their paint. Dandi has written books for all ages, including Little Blessings books, *Degrees of Guilt: Kyra's Story*, *Degrees of Betrayal: Sierra's Story*, *Love Rules*, *Maggie's Story*, the Starlight Animal Rescue series, and the bestselling Winnie the Horse Gentler series. Her books (about 450 titles) have sold more than 4 million copies. She writes and rides from rural Ohio.

Visit Dandi at www.dandibooks.com.

Backyard Horses
Read more about Ellie and her horse adventures in the Backyard Horses series.
Horse Dreams
Backyard Horses
Dandi Daley Mackall
author of the bestselling Winnie the Horse Gentler series
All 4 books now available!
#1 Horse Dreams #2 Cowboy Colt
#3 Chasing Dream #4 Night Mare
www.tyndale.com/kids
CP0471